To Sara —
Shine the beauty
of your Heartlight
bright in the
unique way
only you
can!
Be you !

Deborah

Heartlight Girls™

Beauty's Secret

A Girl's Discovery of Inner Beauty

Beauty's Secret

A Girl's Discovery of Inner Beauty

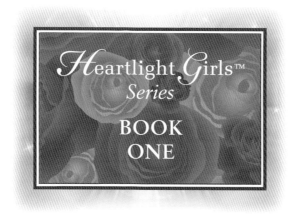

By Debra Gano
Illustrated by Dawn Pitre

Denver, Colorado

♥ ♥

BEAUTY'S SECRET: A Girl's Discovery of Inner Beauty
Heartlight Girls Series Book One

For information, please contact:

Heartlight Girls
P.O. Box 370546
Denver, CO 80237
Toll free: (888)-330-GLOW (4569)
Email: info@HeartlightGirls.com
www.HeartlightGirls.com

Publisher's Cataloging-In-Publication Data
Gano, Debra.
Beauty's secret / Debra Gano; Illustrated by Dawn Pitre. – 1st ed.
p. : col. ill. ; cm. – (Heartlight Girls ; 1)
ISBN: 978-0-9787689-0-4

1. Girls–Juvenile fiction. 2. Self-esteem–Juvenile fiction. 3. Angels–Juvenile fiction. 4. Body image in adolescence–Juvenile fiction. 5. Girls–Fiction. 6. Self-esteem–Fiction. 7. Angels–Fiction. I. Pitre, Dawn. II. Title.

PZ7.G36 Be 2007
[Fic] 2007922904

Designed by Lisa Conner/ Matchbox Studio

Printed on acid-free paper in China by Oceanic Graphic Printing, Inc.
10 9 8 7 6 5 4 3 2

Quotations: Deepak Chopra, excerpted by permission from *The Book of Secrets*, published by Random House, Inc.; Sanaya Roman, excerpted by permission from *Soul Love: Awakening Your Heart Centers*, published by H J Kramer; Elisabeth Kübler-Ross, permission given by the Elisabeth Kübler-Ross Foundation, www.ekrfoundation.org.

♥ Special Thanks

Abundant gratitude goes out to all who believed in the message of this book and helped make it a reality. To illustrator, Dawn Pitre, for your dedication, patience, and spectacular art that brought Beauty's Secret to life; and to book designer, Lisa Conner of Matchbox Studio, for bringing it together so beautifully and with such enthusiasm. Dorsey Moore and Charol Messenger, your editing assistance and wonderful ideas were invaluable. Gina Otto, you have been a remarkable inspiration, role model, mentor, and friend. Thank you for sharing your light and showing me what is possible. To Beth Asbury, Ellie Bryant, Kitty Connell, Cynthia James, and Philip Wyers for the additional input you offered. Each of you made a remarkable difference. To friends and family, especially my parents, who stood by and offered love and support, I thank you with all my heart. And to Dominic Testa, for providing unwavering encouragement, guidance, support, and love. To you I am forever grateful and thank you so much.

My acknowledgments would not be complete without mentioning the overwhelming gratitude I have for my many spiritual teachers over the years. Their inspiration helped me to remember the light within, and I am thankful that now I, too, can be a messenger of this light. *—Debra Gano*

♥ ♥

Contents

Author's Note

Each of us is born with an eternal essence in our soul, what many call "a spark of the divine." This beautiful light, our true self, remains within us throughout our lives, yet often its radiance dims as it becomes buried under layers of cultural conditioning and false perceptions. We go through our lives believing that who we are, and what will make us happy, can be found externally. In truth, the key to our joy is found within, and has been there all the time.

The Heartlight Girls™ series reminds us of this truth by removing the illusions we often believe to be true, allowing the beautiful light and internal strength of the true self to be revealed fully. The words on the pages of these books come openly from my own heart. I have walked this journey myself, searching many years for this light and strength, only to discover it was within me all along.

It is my passion to bring this awareness to our youth. I firmly believe that by remembering the truth of who they really are, they will be empowered to live life to the fullest. Rather than using their energies to search for something "out there," our children can now resourcefully direct their energy to make their own lives, as well as our planet, a much better place.

I invite you to join me in this mission by supporting positive messages of empowerment and truth. Together we can bring about miraculous changes in the world, and celebrate the inner light that connects us all!

With love and light in my heart,

Debra Gano
Founder, Heartlight Girls

To my Ella,
You truly are a bright light,
beautiful inside and out.

ONE

Meet Beauty

*The perfection of outward loveliness is the soul
shining through its crystalline covering.*
−Jane Porter, English novelist and playwright (1776−1850)

In a town along the ocean, on an evening when the sun painted the sky as it set into the water, a baby girl was born. She smiled immediately, a knowing smile of someone with a secret. More noticeable, however, was the beautiful, brilliant light she radiated.

The baby's mother, a wise and soft-spoken woman, looked admiringly at her daughter and said to the father, "Do you see her glow?"

The father simply nodded, unable to take his eyes from his little girl. Normally a man of many words, known for his sense of humor and tendency to tease, he remained unusually quiet, overtaken by the birth of his daughter.

Then, looking out the window to the setting sun, the mother continued, "The sunset is so beautiful this evening, yet our little girl has a beauty that outshines even the most glorious sunset. I think we should name her *Beauty*."

Again the proud father nodded, and Beauty became her name.

*B*eauty grew up in a house high on a bluff, overlooking the ocean's crystal blue water.

Several times a week, when the skies were clear, her family made a ritual of walking down to the beach at the end of the day to watch the sunset. They called it "the show" because the sun painted dramatic colors across the sky, colors which were then reflected onto the liquid canvas of the water. Each time it was different from the last, and the glorious sight before their eyes never ceased to amaze them.

As the last luminous gleam of the sun melted into the horizon, they clapped their hands in celebration.

"Isn't it pretty?" Beauty asked enthusiastically one evening.

"Hmm, which is more beautiful, the sunset or my little girl?" her father said, giving his seven-year-old daughter a wink. "I'll have to think about that."

"Oh, stop teasing her," Beauty's mother said with a smile. "You know it pales in comparison to our little Beauty. She truly is beautiful, both inside and out."

Then, holding her hand over her daughter's heart, she spoke the words she would repeat often in the years to come. "Remember, Beauty, it's what's inside that counts."

*H*earing these words often during her childhood helped Beauty remember the importance of being a kind and loving person. Anytime anyone needed a favor, or even just a hug, she met the request with a big smile and abundant enthusiasm. Beauty loved to help.

She especially liked being helpful to her younger brother, Zackery. He repeatedly turned to his big sister for support, and each time she assisted him in whatever way she could. She nicknamed him "Little Buddy," and it gave her much joy to watch his face light up every time she called him that.

People were drawn to Beauty because of her sweet and fun-loving nature. Whether in school or in her neighborhood, Beauty never lacked for friends; however, she spent most of her time with her best friend, Crystal. They loved being silly together and one of their favorite activities was dressing up in funny costumes. Sometimes they were princesses, sometimes gypsies, but many times they put together costumes that made no sense at all!

One day, ten-year-old Beauty discovered a treasure at a local costume shop.

"Look!" she said to Crystal, as she held up a pair of bright red clown noses. "We have to get these!"

From that day on, it was rare for the girls to be seen without their clown noses. Unconcerned with the opinions of others or the strange looks people gave them, they wore their noses with confidence and laughed until their stomachs hurt. It was just too much fun being silly!

By age sixteen, Beauty had grown into a beautiful young woman. Although she had typical teenage insecurities about her looks, others noticed her natural poise, sparkling eyes, and brilliant smile.

One day, when Beauty and Crystal were walking in the park, Crystal began taking pictures of everything around her, including Beauty. Following cue, Beauty posed in dramatic, exaggerated ways, sending both girls into a fit of laughter. They were laughing so hard they didn't notice a strange woman with black hair and funny-looking glasses watching them. The woman approached Beauty, peering over the edge of her glasses.

"You do that very well, my dear," said the woman in a raspy voice. "I have something that might be of interest to you."

The woman was the contest coordinator for a popular teen magazine. She explained that they were looking for a new girl to be its spokes-model, representing the magazine in print, as well as making personal appearances. The woman encouraged Beauty to enter.

Since this was one of their favorite magazines, Beauty and Crystal squealed and hugged each other. Then Beauty said to the woman, "I will have to speak with my parents about it."

On the way home, her thoughts shifted from excitement to doubt. Was she tall enough? Should she change her hair? Were her eyes, as her father often teased her about, too far apart? Her mind raced with questions.

TWO

The Mysterious Dream

The recipe for beauty is to have less illusion and more soul.
—Mary Baker Eddy, American author and metaphysician (1821-1910)

With her parents' permission, Beauty decided to enter the contest. She always worked hard at everything she did and wanted to give it her full attention. Winning the contest became her primary focus, and soon she was immersed in preparations for this upcoming event.

It was typical for Beauty to retreat to her room to spend time quietly reading. However, now instead of books, she spent hours poring over magazines, wanting to grasp the latest in beauty tips and fashion.

While the perfect spokesmodel candidate would display a combination of strong qualities, both in personality and looks, Beauty's attention shifted toward her outward appearance. All she could think about were things like her hair and makeup, her clothing, and whether others might notice the flaws she felt she possessed. She became especially concerned with her eyes...*were* they too far apart?

With her focus on all of this, Beauty soon found she didn't have time for the fun things she used to do.

ne evening, while Beauty was practicing posing in the mirror, her mother popped her head through the doorway.

"It's a beautiful evening!" her mother announced. "I've made some sandwiches so we could picnic this evening on the beach while we watch the show. Doesn't that sound like fun?"

"No, I'm going to pass," Beauty replied. "I have more important things to do." Turning back to the mirror, she added under her breath, "Plus, I think it's kind of dumb anyway."

Her mother heard this subtle comment, as mothers often do, and with a look of disappointment honored her daughter's wish to be excluded from the family outing.

The next day, Zackery needed his sister's help building a lemonade stand to raise money for his school trip. It had been Beauty's idea and she had promised to help him with it.

Zackery found Beauty in her room, attempting to put her long, golden-brown hair into a hairstyle she had found in a magazine. She didn't like the way it was turning out and was frustrated.

"Not now, Zack!" she scolded. "Can't you see I'm busy? Go away!"

Zackery lowered his head and closed her door, leaving Beauty alone in front of her mirror.

*T*hat night, Beauty had a dream that a mysterious woman appeared to her.

The beautiful woman had long flowing hair that surrounded a gentle face and wore a white glistening dress. Brilliant golden light encircled her translucent figure.

Upon closer look, it appeared the light radiated from the woman's heart, from the inside out, illuminating the room. She smiled sweetly, repeating the words, *"Remember…remember…remember."*

The magical dream faded and Beauty awoke, feeling peaceful, yet puzzled by its meaning.

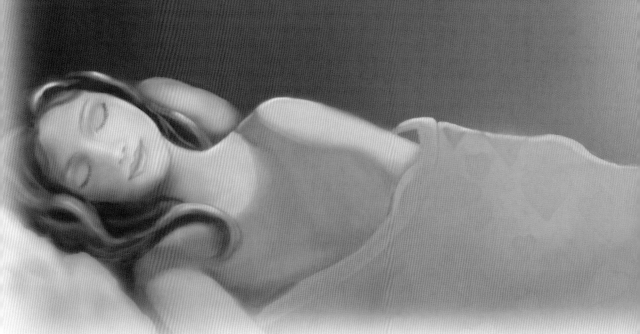

THREE

A Stranger in the Mirror

The only lasting beauty is the beauty of the heart.

– Rumi, Persian poet and theologian (1207-1273)

Remember? Was there something she was supposed to remember? Beauty couldn't think of anything, and soon the mysterious dream faded from her memory.

Although too busy for her family, she always found time to spend with Crystal. The day before the rehearsals, as Beauty and Crystal shopped for Beauty's contest clothing, Crystal's face suddenly lit up.

"Beauty, what if I entered, too? I know it's last minute, but wouldn't it be fun to do together?"

Beauty looked at her in bewilderment. "You? Do you really think you would have a chance?" she scoffed, hoping to discourage her best friend. There had never been any competition between the two, but suddenly Beauty felt threatened.

"Maybe not," answered Crystal, looking a little hurt. "I wasn't even thinking about winning or anything. I was just thinking about how much fun we could have."

"Suit yourself," Beauty said, as a wave of anxiety flooded her. She couldn't help notice Crystal's beautiful eyes and how perfectly spaced they were.

So Crystal and Beauty arrived together for the first day of rehearsal, joined by many other girls. The lady with the funny glasses handed out schedules for the four-day event, and then explained how scores would be accumulated from the categories of poise, personality, attitude and appearance. Upon mention of scores, an uneasy tension filled the room.

"Everyone is so serious here," Crystal whispered to Beauty during rehearsal. "I have an idea! Let's put on our clown noses and pretend we're going to wear them during the contest. It will be a funny joke!"

She giggled and the lady with funny glasses glanced over at them.

Beauty rolled her eyes. "Don't be so silly. I would *never* do that!"

"I was just trying to lighten things up a bit," said Crystal. "You know, Beauty, you're not as much fun as you used to be. Can't you even laugh at yourself anymore?"

Laugh? How could Crystal be having so much fun with this? Beauty thought. *This was serious.*

Crystal shrugged and walked over to a group of girls, leaving Beauty standing alone.

When the day of the contest arrived, Beauty's anxiety peaked. She imagined that whenever anyone looked at her, all they could see were her physical flaws. Magnifying these thoughts in her head, it became difficult for her to concentrate on the contest. With her mind preoccupied and not fully present, she often missed instructions and cues. It began to affect her scores, and her uncertainty rose.

To appear more confident and hide her insecurity, Beauty started talking about the other girls in a negative way, even making fun of them at times. Everyone soon avoided Beauty, which only fueled her insecurities because she didn't understand why she was being avoided. She thought she was being funny.

One of the contestants, a pretty blond girl named Lily, was upset backstage because she couldn't remember the steps to the routine they had practiced at rehearsal. She teetered on the verge of tears.

Crystal noticed this and approached her, offering to help. As Crystal began to show Lily the steps of the routine, Beauty suddenly marched over and firmly pulled her away from Lily.

"Why are you helping her?" demanded Beauty. "She's our competition! You should let her make a mistake!"

"She needs help," Crystal answered, pushing one of her dark, springy curls out of her face, "and I'm going to help her."

Then Crystal added, "Gosh, Beauty, how can you be so mean? What's happened to you? I don't even know who you are anymore."

She shook her head and returned to Lily, leaving Beauty alone again.

*L*ater that afternoon, the lady with the funny-looking glasses made an announcement to the contestants.

"Tomorrow is our last day. Each of you will have a chance to speak and share something special about yourself. This is an important part of the contest and will be scored heavily. The judges would like to know the *real* you. Please prepare and be creative; you may even want your wardrobe to reflect something that is an expression of who you are."

Then she named the contestants with the highest scores so far.

Beauty's name was not mentioned...but Crystal's was!

Beauty was stunned. She glared at Crystal and stormed over to the lady with the funny glasses. "How can Crystal's score be higher than mine? *I'm* the one you asked to be in the contest!"

"I realize this is a surprise for you, Beauty," the woman responded. "However, the judges said that as they got to know Crystal, they saw a special beauty in her, a certain glow about her. They love her smile and the sparkle in her eyes, the way she seems so comfortable with herself. They've also noticed how kind and helpful she always is."

The woman glanced at the roses decorating the stage and breathed in their scent. "Don't they smell beautiful? The true delight of a rose comes from more than its appearance. Remember, Beauty, it's not always just about how you look."

etting even more frustrated, Beauty rolled her eyes and ignored the woman's words. *I wish Crystal had never entered this contest!* she thought as she rushed home to her room, desperate to find something to wear for the final day.

"I just *have* to win!" Beauty said out loud, ignoring an uncomfortable empty feeling that seemed to appear often these days. "Then I'll be happy."

She tried on outfit after outfit, looking at herself in the mirror, feeling critical of herself and everything she tried on. The pile of clothing on the floor was up to her knees. Not liking anything she saw, she gave up on the clothing and moved to her makeup. Maybe new lipstick would be the answer. Then Beauty realized...it must be her eyes! The judges must have thought her eyes *were* too far apart, just like her dad had always teased her. She reached for her eye makeup, determined to find a solution.

Zackery could not have picked a worse time to stop by and ask for help.

Angry and frustrated, Beauty spun from her mirror and yelled, "I don't care about your stupid lemonade stand, Zack! I told you, LEAVE ME ALONE!"

Zack's eyes welled with tears and he closed Beauty's door, leaving her amidst her piles of clothing and tubes of makeup. She turned back to the mirror and was shocked by the unfamiliar face looking back at her.

In place of her sweet, beautiful face glared a mean and ugly one.

Terror filled Beauty. *Who is this? Who am I??*

FOUR

The Angel's Visit

The less you open your heart to others, the more your heart suffers.
−Deepak Chopra, Indian physician and best-selling author

Frightened, Beauty ran out of the house and down the hill to the beach she had known so well since she was a little girl. There she dropped to her knees, buried her head in her hands, and cried.

Beauty had always loved the beach, for it was a special place for her, especially at this time of day.

The sun was just beginning its evening set and cast a rainbow of colors across the sky. The golden sunbeams created glistening sparkles on the water that danced with the rhythmic movement of the gentle waves. The tranquility that takes place at sunset, when the activities of the day subside, thins the veil that separates this world from the one of magic.

Yet on this day, with her head in her hands, Beauty never even noticed the grandeur that surrounded her.

$\mathcal{S}$uddenly, the sun's rays intensified and the waters calmed. Slowly, Beauty looked up. Squinting through her tears, she saw the glowing figure of a woman walking toward her, seemingly out of nowhere. The woman's dress looked like white translucent light, with sparkling golden rays that were magnified by the brilliance of the setting sun. The dress glistened and billowed softly in the wind. The woman's long hair flowed, and around her neck she wore a heart pendant.

As this mystical woman came closer, Beauty could feel the love and kindness she radiated, and sensed a familiar quality about her. Then it occurred to Beauty...this was the woman from her dream!

*P*eacefulness flooded Beauty and she knew this woman as a friend. She instantly felt comfortable confiding in her.

"I'm an awful, ugly person!" Beauty blurted, as raindrop tears streamed down her face. "I don't feel like *me* anymore! What's happened to me?"

"You have forgotten who you are, my dear." The woman stopped in front of Beauty. "That is why I am here."

"Who are you?" Beauty looked up at the mysterious woman and blinked back her tears.

"I am the Heartlight Angel. I have a secret to share with you."

An angel? A secret? Beauty couldn't believe it!

"The secret will remind you of who you truly are," stated the angel.

"What do you mean?" Beauty asked.

The angel explained. "It's wonderful that you take good care of yourself, Beauty, and that you tend to your appearance. These things are important.

"More important, however, is the care you give yourself on the inside. It's important to remember that who you *truly* are goes deeper than your face and your body. They are wonderful gifts, but the real you is so much more than your image."

The angel leaned closer, and her eyes captivated Beauty. They were the color of the sea, green with a small heart-shaped dot in the left one.

"The beauty that comes from inside of you is much more important than what people see on the outside of you," said the angel. "Your *inner* beauty is what the world wants to see."

"I thought people only cared about what I look like on the outside," said Beauty, puzzled. "How do I get inner beauty?"

"You already have it, my dear," replied the Heartlight Angel. "You always have, and you always will. You are born with it, and so is everyone in this world. Inner beauty is what makes everyone on the planet a beautiful being. It is your essence, your *true* self."

"Essence?" asked Beauty. "What's that?"

"It is the beauty inside of you that is constant and never changes. Beautiful qualities like love, joy, peace, harmony, goodness, and grace. These qualities are the *truth* of who you are."

The angel continued. "There is a beautiful bright light that glows within your heart. It is called your *Heartlight.* It is in this special place that you hold these wonderful qualities, Beauty."

With a smile, the Heartlight Angel asked, "Are you ready for the secret?"

Was she ready? Beauty still couldn't believe an angel was delivering a secret to her. She paused momentarily, and then nodded with excitement as the angel revealed her message.

"When you forget about your essence, and these beautiful qualities that define who you *truly* are, your Heartlight grows dim. When your Heartlight is dim, the radiant light inside of you cannot shine forth. Without inner beauty shining brightly, outer beauty quickly dims.

"This is what happens when you are not your *true* self. And when you are your false self, it doesn't feel very good, does it?"

"No, it doesn't," admitted Beauty, casting her eyes down toward the sand.

"Then let's get you feeling better!" the angel said. "Let's get your Heartlight glowing again."

"How do we do that?" asked Beauty.

"Easily. Close your eyes. Slowly, breathe in deeply, and now exhale fully. Do this several times until you feel peaceful." Beauty did this, and the gentle rhythm of the waves helped her to relax.

The angel waited. "Now bring your attention to the center of your chest. Continue breathing and become aware of a light within your heart. It might feel dim at first, but as you focus and recognize its presence, it becomes brighter. Notice the warmth, then remind yourself of the beauty of all the wonderful things inside of you, such as joy, peace, and strength. This is your *true* essence, the real you where inner beauty lies.

"Once you are aware of this presence, you can then feel your Heartlight growing bigger and brighter, radiating out into the world."

The angel paused, letting Beauty enjoy the experience for a while. Then she said softly, "It's a beautiful feeling, isn't it?"

Beauty could only nod and smile, for she was too moved to speak.

FIVE

A Priceless Gift

When you possess light within, you see it externally.

—Anaïs Nin, American writer and diarist (1903-1977)

"Now you know the secret," whispered the Heartlight Angel to Beauty, whose smile grew bigger as her Heartlight became brighter. Slowly Beauty opened her eyes.

"Your Heartlight is again glowing brightly," confirmed the angel.

"Can people see this light?" asked Beauty.

"Others can see it by your kindness, your laughter, and the sparkle in your eyes...as well as feel its presence within you. Believe me, when your Heartlight is glowing brightly, others can't help but notice!"

The angel continued. "And about the contest...don't worry what you will wear, for the most important thing you can wear is a smile. What you wear ear to ear is much more important than what you wear head to toe.

"But in case you were wondering," she added with a wink, "you will have the perfect dress. That's the magic of connecting to your Heartlight... these things take care of themselves!"

*T*he Heartlight Angel turned to look at the sun nearing the horizon. Beauty's eyes followed hers.

"Think of the sunsets you love, Beauty," said the angel. "That beautiful golden light is always there, even on the cloudy days. That's how your Heartlight is — always there, even when it feels clouded over. It is up to you to remind yourself daily of its presence. Quietly go within yourself and make that connection, then allow the light to shine forth. Remember, without inner beauty shining brightly, outer beauty quickly dims."

The angel opened her hands and a shimmering golden bag appeared. "A reminder of my visit," she said, setting the bag next to Beauty.

Then, cradling Beauty's hands in hers, the angel looked lovingly into her eyes. Beauty sensed the angel would be leaving soon.

"Thank you for everything!" said Beauty. "You've given me such wonderful gifts."

"The gift of light was always yours, Beauty. You just had to go within yourself to find it. Please remember this secret, and know this is a secret meant to be shared."

Then the angel leaned closer, and with one last smile, whispered sweetly, "Always…remember your *Heartlight*."

As the angel said these words, her own Heartlight became brighter and brighter until it was so intense, Beauty had to close her eyes.

When she opened them, the angel was gone.

*L*ost in her thoughts, Beauty remained on the beach, as one realization after another occurred.

"Now I know why my scores at the contest are so low," she said to a nearby seagull attempting to nap on the beach. "I've been ignoring the most important part of me!" Beauty realized that her self-esteem had become really low because she was focusing so much on her external self and what other people thought of her. She often criticized herself and others, and didn't like the person she had become.

Then it made sense. "How could anyone think I was beautiful with the awful way I've been acting?" she asked the seagull, who actually seemed to be listening this time. Beauty shuddered, remembering the many times she ignored her family and friends or harshly judged others. Then she thought of the beauty everyone saw in Crystal, recognizing the inner light the angel described.

"Crystal's Heartlight must really be bright," she confided to her seaside pal. "That's why she always seems so happy." Beauty recalled her own unhappiness, now understanding that empty feeling that gnawed away at her so often. Her dim Heartlight affected not only others, but how she felt about herself. Forgetting about the light and love in her heart caused her to look to the outside world to fill a void she now knew could only be filled by her own love and appreciation of herself.

"I will change this!" Beauty declared loudly to the departing seagull. "I'll never again make my outer self more important than my inner self, I promise!"

As the sun blushed at the ocean's edge, Beauty focused again on the light in her heart. She felt its warmth, and a brilliant glow radiated out from her.

She smiled, realizing it was the most beautiful sunset she had ever seen.

SIX

Message on the Scroll

Look at yourself through your soul's eyes. See the beauty of your being.
– Sanaya Roman, American author

*D*usk settled in and Beauty jumped up, full of joy. She grabbed the bag given to her by the Heartlight Angel, and began the climb back to her house.

On her way, she saw her family walking hand in hand after their evening of watching the sunset at the beach. They were talking and laughing, but when they saw Beauty, they stopped suddenly.

Her mother sensed something different about her daughter. From being sullen and withdrawn, Beauty suddenly possessed a vibrant and glowing quality. "You look absolutely radiant!" her mother said.

Casting his daughter a curious glance, her father added, "Would you care to explain what you have been up to?"

"Just remembering who I am!" Beauty said, beaming.

Then, giving each of them an enthusiastic hug, she added, "That's all!"

Beauty took her little brother's hand and, as a family, they returned home.

After laughing and having fun with her family, Beauty couldn't wait to go to her room to open the mysterious golden bag. She held her breath in anticipation.

Slowly she untied the silken cords that held it closed, revealing a box with a gold ribbon around it. Beauty carefully untied the ribbon and opened the box. Inside was a beautiful necklace with a heart pendant, just like the one the Heartlight Angel was wearing!

Then, Beauty noticed something unusual at the bottom of the bag. She reached in and, to her surprise, pulled out a scroll. As she unrolled the delicate paper, a beautiful handwritten message appeared. It read...

"True beauty lies within.
Know how beautiful you are,
always...
Remember your Heartlight
and let your light shine!"

Aware she had made her insecurities bigger than they really were, that they were simply an illusion she had blown out of proportion, Beauty again went to her mirror, the one that had earlier frightened her so. Reflected back to her now was a beautiful girl, with a radiant smile and sparkling eyes. Eyes that were hers, perfect and beautiful just the way they were.

Suddenly sleepy, she climbed into bed, with the new necklace around her neck, a smile on her face, and a glowing light within her heart.

True beauty lies within.
Know how beautiful you are,
always...
Remember your Heartlight
and let your light shine!

*M*orning dawned, and an intuitive hunch to open her bedroom closet awakened Beauty. There, shimmering and glistening in iridescent colors, was the most beautiful dress she had ever seen. Yet the most special thing about it was the way the sparkles picked up the light and formed the word *"LOVE"* all over it.

It was perfect for the contest, because love was exactly what Beauty felt, both for herself and for others as well.

She thought of her friend, the Heartlight Angel...*I'm so grateful for her visit, I'll never forget it!* Beauty knew that, by remembering the truth of who she truly was, she could make smarter decisions and wiser choices. She would no longer hurt the people she loved...including herself.

Suddenly, it occurred to Beauty that it didn't even matter whether she won the contest or not. It seemed so important before, but now, with a new sense of peace, it didn't even seem that big of a deal.

"Crystal sure had the right idea about doing this contest for fun!" said Beauty to herself, as she rummaged through her dresser drawer, trying to find her clown noses. She realized that by being so attached to winning, she had taken all the joy out of the event. She decided to let go of the outcome and simply enjoy herself. She looked forward to being her silly self again.

Excited about the contest, she prepared for the many things she had to do. Then she recalled the angel's advice: *"Connect with your Heartlight every day."* Beauty knew this was the most important preparation she had to do.

And she knew exactly where she needed to go.

SEVEN

A Secret Revealed

People are like stained-glass windows.
They sparkle and shine when the sun is out, but when the darkness sets in,
their true beauty is revealed only if there is a light from within.

– Elisabeth Kübler-Ross, Swiss-American psychiatrist and author (1926-2004)

After her quiet time on the beach connecting with her Heartlight, Beauty returned home, feeling empowered and much more confident.

She gathered together her dress, the heart necklace, and her shoes for the contest that evening. She put the clown noses into her purse, and then remembered the scroll. Beauty slipped it in as well, silently reminding herself to read it throughout the day.

Upon leaving, she saw Zackery painting his lemonade stand in the garage. He was covered head to toe in paint. Although tight on time, Beauty picked up a paintbrush. "Need any help, Little Buddy?"

Zack happily accepted and together they finished the job quickly. Then he giggled, and Beauty laughed, too, when she realized she was also covered with paint.

"Oh well!" she said, grinning and giving her face a wipe. Then hugging her brother, she added, "First thing tomorrow, we're open for business!"

On her way to the contest, Beauty noticed a very strange thing.

Suddenly everything seemed to glow with brilliance, as if her eyes were open for the first time. She could now see the light and beauty in everything: the glorious nature around her, the people she met, even the little animals that scurried along her path. She realized that all things had an inner beauty that she hadn't noticed before.

This put a big smile on her face, and when she arrived at the contest her new glow was obvious. Everyone gathered around her.

Beauty wanted to share her discovery, but knew she had something very important to do first.

She set out to find Crystal.

"I'm sorry I've been acting so awful lately," Beauty said when she found her.

"Apology accepted," Crystal grinned, relieved to have her best friend back.

Then, giving Beauty a curious look, she added, "Something's different about you. What is it?"

"I remembered what *really* counts," said Beauty with a new confidence. "I'll never let you down again, I promise."

Then, opening her hand to reveal their clown noses, Beauty giggled and said, "Friends?"

Crystal laughed. "Friends."

They hugged and together said, "*Forever!*"

*E*vening approached and the audience arrived to watch the big event. The lights dimmed and a hush filled the room. The contest began and soon it was Beauty's turn to say a few words about herself.

She took a few deep breaths, remembering the guidance of the Heart-light Angel. As she focused on her inner beauty, the light in Beauty's heart began to glow. She knew the words she was about to speak would come from a place deep within her heart.

"This contest has given me a chance to learn," she began, "that life is not all about our outward appearance. We can take really good care of how we look, but if we don't take care of ourselves on the inside, our outside shows it.

"If we are not beautiful on the inside, there is nothing beautiful about us. Our inner beauty is who we *truly* are, and it is so much more important than how we look on the outside.

"Letting our inner light shine through is important," she continued, "because *that's* the part of us the world wants to see!"

She smiled and her face was radiant. Glancing at her family sitting in the audience, Beauty could tell how proud they were of her. Then, locking eyes with her mother and feeling her love, she suddenly recalled the words from her childhood.

"Like my mom always said," Beauty added, "'it's what's inside that counts!'"

Beauty's eyes sparkled and the glow from her heart illuminated the darkened room.

Everyone noticed, especially the judges.

"We have a most unusual situation here," said one of the judges before announcing the winner. "In addition to awarding our first place winner a contract with the magazine, we have decided to offer a second contract as well." A stir of excitement filled the room, as both audience and contestants reacted with curiosity to the change in plans.

"First place goes to…Crystal, our grand prize winner!" said the judge, as the audience cheered. "And our second contract," the judge continued, "goes to a girl who scored so well on this final day that she moved from very far behind into a close second place. Congratulations, Beauty!"

Again the crowd cheered. Beauty hugged Crystal, and told her best friend how truly excited she was for her. As the girls embraced, the glow of their connected Heartlights became magnetic. Soon television and newspaper reporters surrounded them. One reporter asked, "Beauty, you were trailing most of the contest; now you're a winner. How did you do it? Do you have a special beauty secret you can share?"

"I sure do," Beauty beamed, holding a bouquet of roses. "I remembered my Heartlight!"

Then the lady with the funny glasses approached, peering over her glasses in her usual way. As Beauty looked into this woman's eyes, she saw a unique sparkle she hadn't noticed before, and realized that even this odd-looking woman was truly beautiful. Beauty removed one of her roses, sniffed its fragrance, and then handed it to the woman.

"Now I understand," said Beauty, smiling. "Thank you so much."

"I'm very proud of you," the woman said warmly. "You really are beautiful, both inside and out."

*T*he next day, Zack and Beauty began their day of selling lemonade.

Crystal came by, wearing her clown nose. Beauty promptly added hers, found one for Zack, and together the three of them drew enough attention to have a very successful day, raising more than enough money for Zackery to attend his school trip.

Evening approached, and Beauty and her brother joined their parents at the beach to watch the sunset.

As the setting sun cast its radiant brilliance across the sky, Beauty felt its glow upon her face.

Then she smiled and remembered the glow of light within her heart.

Beauty is not in the face. Beauty is a light in the heart.

-Khalil Gibran, Syrian poet, writer and painter (1883-1931)

$\mathcal{H}$EARTLIGHT $\mathcal{M}$EDITATION
To Connect With Your Inner Beauty

Want to connect with your Heartlight?
It's fun, easy, and only takes a few minutes!

Here's how:

1. You can connect with your Heartlight anywhere, at anytime, but it's helpful if you're alone (or do with a friend) and in a quiet place. If possible, choose a place that is special for you, a place you find peaceful. It could be a park, a garden, by a lake, your backyard, or even your bedroom (be sure to close the door).

2. Sit or lie quietly, close your eyes, and begin the process by just breathing. See how easy this is?

3. Take a deep breath in, and then exhale fully. Do this a few times until your body and mind feel peaceful. If you've had an especially stressful day, imagine yourself breathing out all of this stress as you exhale. Visualize it as a dark cloud leaving your body.

4. Now place your attention on the center of your chest. This is where your Heartlight is. Imagine a spark of light there, and as you put your thoughts there, this spark begins to glow and get brighter. You feel you have a warm ball of light in your chest.

5. Remind yourself of the beautiful qualities you hold there, like love, joy, peace, beauty and wisdom. Say to yourself, silently or out loud, *"I am beautiful, inside and out."*

6. Continue breathing and imagine this ball of light expanding, becoming bigger and bigger, until it surrounds your entire body.

7. Now imagine this light becoming brighter and brighter, so bright that its rays extend out from you into the world as far as you can imagine! Say to yourself, again either silently or out loud, *"I am a beautiful bright light shining out into the world."* Radiate this light daily and see how beautiful your world can be!

Remember your Heartlight and let your light shine!

Heartlight Girls™

Empowering Girls from the Inside Out

At *Heartlight Girls*, we are dedicated to the empowerment
of girls everywhere. Our inspirational books and products
bring awareness of the ever-present light within,
developing girls from the inside out, at the core,
where self-esteem begins.

To experience more of the Heartlight Girls magic,
please visit :

www.HeartlightGirls.com

*Heartlight Girls donates a portion of book sales
to organizations that support the empowerment of girls.*